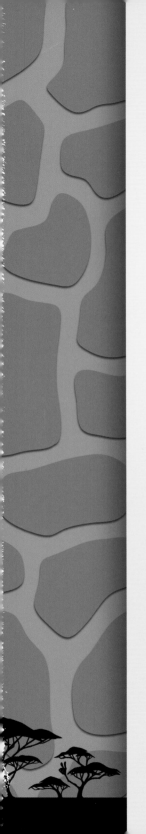

CURIOSITY CRESCENT

AN *Audrey Amaka* STORY

WRITTEN AND ILLUSTRATED BY

BRENT VERNON

Dedicated to my parents, George & Ruthie Vernon, who faithfully and lovingly taught me the importance of obedience and responsibility.

ISBN 978-0-9831638-1-7   Visit us online at *WWW.BRENTVERNON.COM*

Audrey Amaka did not have a neck like other giraffes. In fact, she didn't have a neck at all! But what she *did* have was brain power—and lots of it! Everyone knew that Audrey Amaka had a good head on her shoulders.

Audrey was an excellent student. She loved every single subject in school, but—most of all—she loved *geography*.

"I want to see the world!" Audrey announced to her class one afternoon during study time.

"I'm sure you *will* see the world, Audrey," said Miss Nell, her teacher. "But next time, please get permission to speak out in class."

"Yes, ma'am," said Audrey, her cheeks turning pink.

Audrey's class was studying a part of the country known as "Curiosity Crescent," a mysterious region famous for its natural wonders—brilliant and unusual wonders.

Audrey became fascinated with the Crescent and read every book she could find about this strange and beautiful place.

One afternoon, while Audrey was in the living room doing homework with her friends Nelson and Doodle, Mr. Amaka appeared in the doorway.

"How would you like to go on a camping trip?" he asked with a grin.

"*Yaaayyy!*" hollered Audrey. "Wait—who are you talking to?"

"*All* of you!" laughed Mr. Amaka.

"*Yaaaaayyy!*" hollered Doodle, bouncing up and down in his chair.

"Shouldn't we get permission first?" asked Nelson.

"I have already checked with your parents," Mr. Amaka said to the boys. "We are leaving at six o' clock tomorrow morning. Don't be late!"

Audrey frowned. "Are you forgetting that Mom doesn't like to go camping?"

"Your mother is planning to visit Auntie Lou this week, so only the four of us will go. I have some business to manage while we're gone, so you kids will be on your own a couple of times. I expect you to stick together and obey all my instructions."

"Where are we going?" Audrey asked.

"I think you'll like it," said Mr. Amaka. "I am taking you to a place called 'Curiosity Crescent.'"

Audrey's squeal was so loud that it set off the security alarm.

At six o' clock the next morning, the boys arrived at Audrey's house, packed and ready to go. Before they had a chance to knock, the front door swung open and Audrey waddled out, her arms full of suitcases and tote bags. As always, she was wearing her sparkly blue heels.

About that time, Mr. Amaka pulled up with the wagon. "No, ma'am!" he said, looking at Audrey sternly. "This trip is only four days long. Take no more than what you need."

"But *Daaaaaad!*" Audrey whined.

"You heard me," said Mr. Amaka. "Remember? Obedience."

As the wagon bounced along the dirt road, Audrey and the boys watched the sun rise.

"Can you believe it?" Audrey sighed dreamily. "We're on our way to Curiosity Crescent—the land of a thousand wonders!"

"I think *you* are a wonder, Audrey," said Doodle.

"What kind of wonders?" asked Nelson.

"The big kind!" Audrey gushed. "Huge trees, giant beehives, and super tall waterfalls! It's all so fantastic."

It was late in the day when Mr. Amaka pulled the wagon onto a plateau overlooking a lush green valley.

"Are we *here?*" Audrey asked anxiously. "Is this Curiosity Crescent?"

"We are on the edge of the Crescent," said Mr. Amaka. "This is where we make camp."

The kids cheered and scrambled out of the wagon.

"What a view!" yelled Doodle, hopping with excitement.

8

"Listen up, everyone," said Mr. Amaka. "I'll be away on business tomorrow, but will return before nightfall. The same thing will happen the next day. This valley is a safe place and has many wonderful things for you to do while I'm gone. But you *must not* wander beyond the valley floor. Is that clear?"

"Yes, sir," said the kids.

"Good," said Mr. Amaka. "Now... let's set up some tents!"

Audrey woke up the next morning to the sound of her father's voice.

"I'm leaving now, Audrey," he said, standing just outside her tent. "Have a good day and remember to be careful. I love you *so* much."

"Okay, Dad," said Audrey. "I love you, too."

When the sound of his footsteps faded away, Audrey dressed and crawled out into the morning light.

"Are you awake in there?" she hollered over to the boys' tent.

"I'm not," said Doodle, stifling a giggle, "and neither is Nelson."

"I have big plans for us today," said Audrey. "I am taking you to see *Buluu*, a giant baobab tree. We need to get back here before Dad does, so let's get moving!"

The boys poked their heads out of their tent and looked at Audrey in disbelief.

"Is this *Buluu* thing beyond the valley floor?" asked Nelson. "Why can't we stay here and play Hide-n-Seek like normal kids?"

"Look," said Audrey, placing her hands on her hips, "we may never get a chance to come here again. You don't want to miss this!"

It was a beautiful day for a hike, but the boys were nervous.

"I feel guilty," said Doodle, wiping his forehead.

"I do, too!" said Nelson. "We should be obeying your dad, Audrey."

"You guys have been whining all morning," said Audrey. "Take my word for it; you will love this!"

Audrey wasn't kidding. Just around the next corner, they saw it— bright and blue and towering high into the heavens.

"*Buluu!*" gasped Audrey in amazement.

"*Buluu!*" echoed the boys, just as amazed.

The afternoon flew by as Audrey, Nelson, and Doodle studied the giant baobab, circling the base of its massive trunk and examining its brightly colored branches.

Doodle was especially impressed. "For the first time ever," he whispered, "I feel *small*."

Around the campfire that evening, Mr. Amaka looked at Audrey and the boys intently. "What did you kids do today?" he asked.

Audrey sipped her hot cocoa and stared at the ground. Nelson inspected his claws while Doodle pretended to fall asleep.

After a long pause, Mr. Amaka cleared his throat. "Well?"

"We didn't do much," said Audrey, swallowing hard. "We just played Hide-n-Seek in the valley. How was your day, Dad?"

As soon as Mr. Amaka left the next morning, Audrey convinced Nelson and Doodle to go exploring with her again.

"Where are we going this time?" asked Doodle as they were leaving the campsite.

"The Hives of Kifaru," said Audrey. "You won't believe what the local honey bees have created!"

Nelson stopped in his tracks. "Do you mean *killer bees?*"

"Well, yes," said Audrey. "But they're not too dangerous unless you upset them."

"I don't think this is a good idea," said Nelson, looking pale. "And your dad would be so upset if he knew what we were doing."

Audrey rolled her eyes. "We didn't get caught before, did we?"

16

The boys followed Audrey through the hills and across a dry river bed. Before long, they found themselves in a dusty field of nutgrass and thorn bushes. *And music.*

"What is that sound?" asked Doodle, his ears perking up.

17

"More importantly," gulped Nelson, "what is that *thing?*"

In the middle of the field stood a massive rhinoceros—a fearsome form against the hazy afternoon sky.

"The Hives of Kifaru!" said Audrey excitedly.

Nelson stared at her. "I don't understand," he said. "There's a huge rhino in front of us... and you're happy about it?"

"This place has a great vibe!" said Doodle, tapping his toes.

"That music," giggled Audrey, "is the song of the honey bees. And that rhino isn't really a rhino at all. That's just a bunch of beehives *shaped* like a rhino. Isn't it grand?"

Before the boys had a chance to say anything, Audrey grabbed their hands and pulled them toward the hives.

"Let's get a better look!" she laughed, yanking them along.

Up close, the hives were even more astonishing. The bees had sculpted the rhinoceros perfectly. Every detail was in place.

"And they hum pretty, too," said Doodle, still jigging to the music.

"Calm down, Doodle!" said Nelson. "You might upset the bees!"

Doodle snorted. "Look who's talking," he said playfully. "I'm not the clumsy one here. Remember the snake's nest?"

"Hey guys, check this out!" whispered Audrey as she tiptoed between the rhinoceros' feet. "It's like a cave under here!

As the boys crept into the shadow of the hives, something terrible happened! Nelson tripped on one of the rhinoceros' giant toenails and fell hard, slamming into the statue's right front leg.

Audrey and Doodle watched in horror as the leg caved in, causing the whole structure to lean.

"*RUN!*" Audrey screamed. And run they did.

As the kids scattered, the Hives of Kifaru buckled
and crashed to the ground. Like a volcanic eruption, a churning
black cloud exploded from the crumbling rhinoceros—African honey
bees. *Angry* African honey bees. *Killer bees!*

23

Audrey woke up in a gully with her feet in the air. Her jumper was torn and her tail was knotted. Worst of all, the heels of her sparkly blue shoes were broken.

"No, no, *NO!!*" she wailed, *"This is a travesty!"*

Nelson was lying a short distance away. While making his escape, he had stumbled over a clump of nutgrass and landed in the gully.

"I think I broke my arm," he moaned. "It's the third time!" He propped himself up to look around. "Where's Doodle?"

"Ober here," said a mournful voice. "In da brambles."

Audrey and Nelson hobbled to a nearby thorn bush and carefully pulled back a few of the branches. They gasped.

"I tried to distract da bees," said Doodle. He smiled weakly.

"Oh, Doodle," said Audrey with tears in her eyes, "you're a mess!"

Poor Doodle *was* a mess. In his attempt to keep Audrey and Nelson safe, he had been stung dozens of times. From the top of his head to the soles of his feet, he was blistered, swollen, and badly scratched.

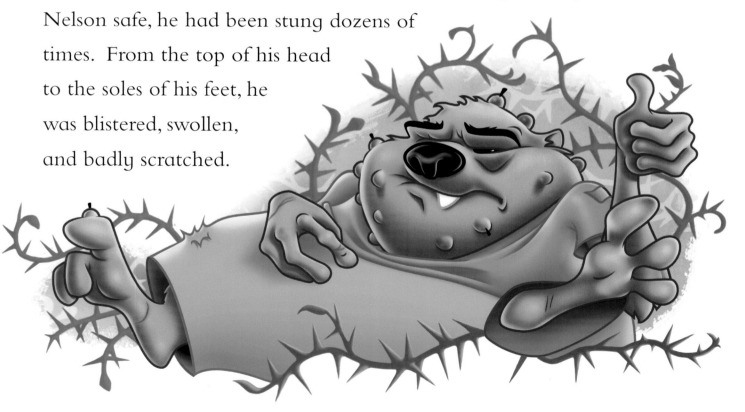

It was long past sundown when the tattered trio finally arrived back at the campsite.

Mr. Amaka was overwrought. *"Where have you kids been?"* he bellowed. "I've been worried sick!"

"We left the valley today," blurted Audrey, bursting into tears. "And yesterday too. I just *had* to go exploring!"

Mr. Amaka noticed that the boys were hurt. He wasted no time making a sling for Nelson's broken arm and tending to Doodle's bee stings, spreading cool mud on the swollen areas.

"It was my fault," continued Audrey. "I made the boys go with me."

"It was our fault too," added Nelson.

"But *I* caused this breach of trust," Audrey wailed. "I disobeyed. And then I lied about it." By now, her sobs were loud enough to wake the valley floor. *"I'm so sorry, Dad!"*

"Cud sumbutty tell me what a 'breach of trust' is?" asked Doodle.

"I am very disappointed in all three of you," said Mr. Amaka. "I thought I could trust you to follow my instructions."

"Audrey, I am especially disappointed in you. You have the gift of intelligence. But with every gift comes the responsibility to use it wisely. This gift should never be used as an excuse for bad behavior. *Always* obey your parents—even when you don't agree with the rules."

"Yes, sir," whimpered Audrey.

"I was planning a big surprise for you kids tomorrow," said Mr. Amaka, "but because of your disobedience, I'll have to cancel most of it."

"What was the surprise?" asked Nelson.

"I made arrangements for the Black Herons to take you on a sky tour of the entire region, with special stops in the Akoko Ravine, on the Fields of St. Alvin, and on the Shani Peaks."

Audrey knew all about these wonderful places. Deeply disappointed, she started to sniffle again. "So... are we just gonna go home?"

"Not yet," said Mr. Amaka.

At dusk the following evening, Mr. Amaka pulled the wagon into a crowded meadow at the foot of an enormous waterfall.

"Camilla Falls!" whooped Audrey as she recognized the crown jewel of Curiosity Crescent sparkling in the African twilight.

"Why is this place so packed?" asked Nelson.

"Oh, you'll see!" said Audrey. She winked at her dad.

Before long, the evening sky came to life with dancing lights.

Everyone cheered as a colorful meteor shower illuminated the Falls.

Weeks later, Audrey was still talking about the Lights on Camilla.

"It was amazing, Mom! That happens every twenty-six years... and we got to see it!"

"That's wonderful, darling," said Mrs. Amaka.

"Dad said that, next time, we're gonna spend a whole week in Curiosity Crescent... if I obey the rules. Which I *will*."

"Oh!" exclaimed Mrs. Amaka. "I almost forgot. Hippo Tim from the shoe shop called. Your heels have been repaired!"

"Yaaayyy!" squealed Audrey. "May I go and pick 'em up?"

"You may," said her mother, "but please come home right away. No detours or adventures this afternoon. It's almost time for dinner."

"Yes, ma'am," said Audrey.

Returning home, Audrey was happy to be wearing her favorite shoes. She was also happy to bump into Nelson and Doodle along the way.

"Wow!" said Audrey. "You guys look great!"

"My swelling is gone," Doodle grinned, "and my wounds are healing."

"And my cast is coming off next week!" said Nelson, holding up his broken arm. He was smiling too, an unusual thing for Nelson.

"I wish we could talk more," said Audrey, "but I'm kinda in a hurry."

"That's too bad," said Doodle. "We thought you might want to join us for a make up game of Hide-n-Seek."

"That sounds like fun," said Audrey, "but I have instructions to go home right away. And we all know how important it is to obey, right?"

The boys smiled again, nodded, and waved goodbye.

So it was that Audrey Amaka, an intelligent little giraffe, learned to obey. Not only that, Audrey learned to use her head *wisely*. From there on out, she was honest and responsible. And always grateful for her adventure in Curiosity Crescent!

"Children, obey your parents in the Lord, for this is right. Honor your father and mother..."

EPHESIANS 6:1 & 2A

The End

Did you KNOW?

◆   With its massive trunk and spacious cavities, the baobab tree is home to many kinds of insects and animals. Even humans use hollow baobab trunks to store goods and find shelter.

◆   Africanized honey bees are called **killer bees** because of their aggressive behavior. Their stings are painful, but are no more deadly than the sting of an average honey bee.

◆   A meteor shower takes place when fast-moving space particles enter the earth's atmosphere, become very hot, and burn away. **Meteors**—often called "shooting stars"—are the trails of light created by these burning particles.

Did you NOTICE?

There are a few surprises hidden in this book. Can you find a honey bee wearing roller skates? Did you see any trees waving, pointing, or posing? Be sure to look carefully!